For all our families and friends,
with thanks for their support and encouragement
over the years – H.G. and K.T.

First published in Great Britain in 2005 by
Frances Lincoln Children's Books, 4 Torriano Mews
Torriano Avenue, London NW5 2RZ
www.franceslincoln.com

Distributed in the USA by Publishers Group West

British Library Cataloguing in Publication Data
available on request

ISBN 1-84507-284-7

Set in Stone Sans

Printed in China
1 3 5 7 9 8 6 4 2
Visit Pablo's website at www.pablothelittleredfox.com

Pablo Goes Hunting

Story by Keith Tutt
Pictures by Hannah Giffard

FRANCES LINCOLN CHILDREN'S BOOKS

"I'm hungry," said Pablo.

"So am I," said Poppy.

"Not as hungry as me," said Pumpkin.

Rose looked at her sad little cubs
and wondered when their dad, Red Fox,
would come back.

"Why can't we hunt for our own food
in the city?" Pablo asked.

"You're still too young, cubs," said Rose.
"You wait here, while I go and help
your father."

And she disappeared into the night.

Pablo turned to his brother
and sister. "Come on, you two.
We're going hunting."

"You heard what Mum
told us!" Poppy warned.

"But Pumpkin's hungry –
aren't you, Pumpkin?"

"Very, very hungry," Pumpkin
sniffed.

"The sooner we hunt, the
sooner we'll eat!" Pablo said,
heading out of the den.

Poppy sighed. She really
hoped Pablo wouldn't get
them into trouble again.

Gil Gull looked down from the apple tree.

"Well, well, well! Three little fox cubs, looking for adventure!"

"Actually," Pumpkin said, "we're looking for FOOD."

"How about the rubbish dump where I live?" said Gill.

"No, no, NO!" Pablo said crossly. "We want real hunting! Not just digging about in the dump."

The big gull felt hurt. "Pablo didn't mean it!" said Poppy, as Gil flapped off into the gathering dusk. But she wasn't sure if he'd heard her...

Pablo led the way along the canal
to the bridge.

"There are loads of fish here,"
he said. "You know how much
you like fish, Pumpkin."

"I DO love fish, Pablo.
I really do!"

Everything looked upside down to
Pumpkin as he held on to Pablo's tail.

"Hold tight, Pumpkin! There'll be
a school of fish along any moment
now!"

But Pablo's tail was tickling Pumpkin's
nose, and before he could tell anyone,
he sneezed!

AchooOOO!

Pablo fell in the water with a mighty splash.
Poppy was so shocked that she let go of Pumpkin.
"Noooooo!" he squealed. His little round body
made such a splash that even Poppy was drenched.

"Maybe," said Poppy, "fishing in the canal wasn't such a good idea."

"Well, maybe," said Pablo, trying to think of something clever to say, "maybe... I've got a better idea. Follow me!"

Just around the next corner was a surprise –
more food than the cubs had ever seen in their lives.

They walked up to it, admired it, sniffed it, licked it.

"Time to tuck in!" Pablo said.

But before they could take a single bite…

"Are these YOUR friends?"
Pumpkin's voice was shaking.

Pablo and Poppy looked up.
The growling, dribbling dogs
didn't look much like anybody's
friends – not even each other's.

Pablo looked at the enormous
fish in front of him, and then
at the dogs.

"Run!" Poppy squealed.
"NOW!"

In a moment, all three cubs were running for their lives.

"They'll never catch me here," Pablo thought, as he waited in his hiding-place. Soon he'd run for home and catch up with Poppy and Pumpkin.

Suddenly Pablo was soaring up into the dark
night. He felt as if he were flying. Way below, the
dogs looked up and started barking at him.

"Oh dear," he said to himself, "maybe going
hunting on our own wasn't such a good idea."

Pumpkin and Poppy looked
up at their brother. Pumpkin
could feel tears in his eyes.

"What are we going to do?"

"We'll think of something,"
said Poppy, although she couldn't
really think of anything at all.

But just then she saw
someone familiar…

Was that Pablo? Gil wondered. If it was,
why were all the dogs barking at him?
   "Gil! Help!"
   "Help? After what you said about my dump?"
Gil squawked.

"Please! I've got a beautiful fresh fish!"

The big gull looked at Pablo's enormous catch.

It did look tasty.

"Hold on tight, little red fox!" Gil called, and he
lifted Pablo up over the heads of the angry dogs.

Poppy and Pumpkin were amazed
to see their brother flying through the sky.

The cubs laughed and hooted as Gil and Pablo landed in the garden.

"You're a good friend, Gil," Pumpkin said, as Poppy gave the gull a foxy lick.

"Yuck!" Gil wiped his bill with one of his big grey wings.

"Sorry for being rude about your home, Gil," said Pablo.

"That's OK, Pablo. I know you didn't mean it. Now get back in that den, you crazy cubs. Here come your mum and dad!"

The cubs dived into the den and started chasing each other's tails.
It was good to be home again. Suddenly Pablo stopped.
   "Ooops, I've forgotten something!" But it was too late.

"I searched all over town for our supper," said
Red Fox, as he came into the den, "and guess
where I found half a fish?"

"Half a fish?" asked Pablo, hoping Gil was enjoying
the other half.

"I found it in the garden!" said Red Fox.

The cubs tried to look surprised.

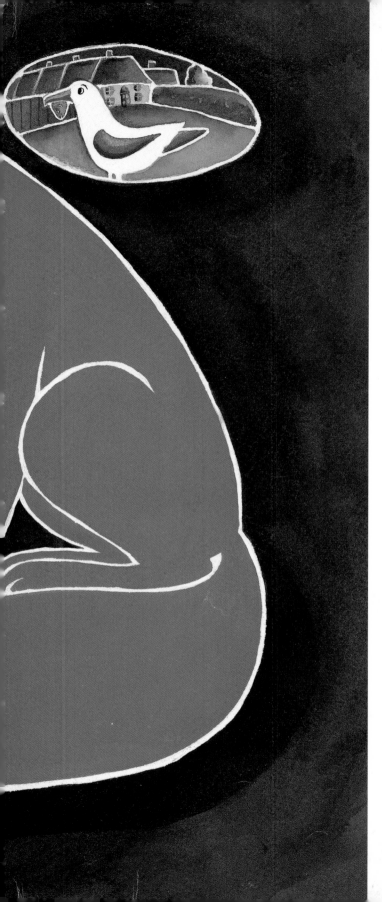

"As you've waited here so patiently," Rose told the cubs, "you can share it between you."

"Perhaps it's best," Pablo whispered to Poppy and Pumpkin, "if we don't tell Mum and Dad how the fish got here."

But Poppy and Pumpkin were far too busy gobbling their supper even to think of answering!